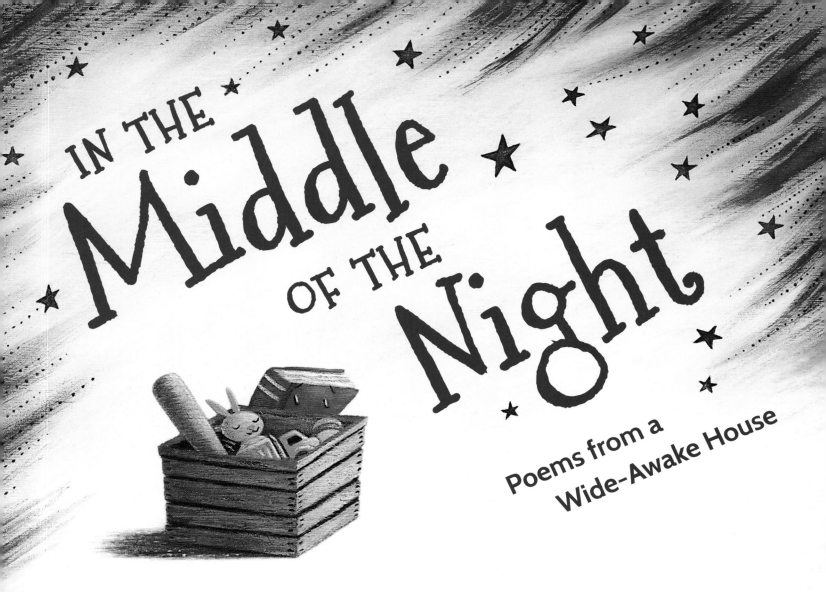

IN THE Middle OF THE Night

Poems from a Wide-Awake House

Laura Purdie Salas

Illustrated by

Angela Matteson

WORD SONG

AN IMPRINT OF HIGHLIGHTS

Honesdale, Pennsylvania

Contents

After Hours

Sun and moon have traded places–
Time for games! Time for races!

We wait,
we wait,
we wait

         all

               day

for **you** to sleep, so we can play!

Your breathing settles, slow and deep.
Finally! You're fast asleep.

Shhhhhhhh . . .

Animals on the Go

Lion flips.
Monkey snips.

Dolphin drums.
Dragon strums.

Hippo rides.
Chameleon hides.

Octopus skates,
juggles plates!

What goes on from dark till dawn?
Animals are on the go
              in . . .

A LATE-NIGHT TALENT SHOW!

7

Lidless Marker's Lament

My head is aching.
Throat feels dry.

My ink fades off
into the sky.

I skip on paper,
scratch and skid.

I'm useless since
you lost my lid.

Take Flight

I crease my edge.
I fold a wedge.
     Got one wing—then, a pair.

I twist and bend.
I dive to send
     myself into the air.

On wings untried,
I dip and glide.
     I loop-de-loop all night.

I'm sharp and sleek—
a paper streak,
     a moonlight midnight flight.

When a Comb Tries to Help

I like things nice and neat,
like my white and tidy teeth.
I comb out Lion's whiskers
'til he shows his fangs beneath.

Kleenex Makes a Perfect Landing

Paper clip skydiver clutches me tight.
I billow like jellyfish in the starlight.
I glide like a kite, like the notes of a flute.
I'm a soft-landing,
        feather-light,
                white parachute!

Baseball Cap Looks for a New Head

I need a comfy place
        to sit.
Globe's too big and bat's too small—
I slide right off your basketball.
But Gigi's curls:
        a perfect fit!

Overdue-Book Hide-and-Seek

I'm not in your backpack.
Or under your bed.
And you HAVE to find me—
Ms. Teabottom said!

I creep to your closet—
I burrow. I sneak.
I LOVE to play overdue-book
hide-and-seek!

Empty Pocket

I'm an empty spot–
      a vacant lot.
I'm alone
      with nothing to do.

Come button, toothpick, pebble, gum–
I'm nothing without
      you!

I'm a treasure chest
      or a robin's nest.
You are jewels
      or eggs, bright blue!

Come nickel, sticker, piece of string,
I'm nothing without
      you!

Dreamy

Pretty and breakable–that's me. But
Every night I dream of
Running, jumping,
Falling lid over bottom, rolling
Under the dresser,
Misting out roses and lavender while I
Explore the world.

UnTIEd!

When he's hot
under the
collar,
I get
the blame.
I'm a pain in
the neck—that's
my claim to fame. I
quit being knotty the
second we're home. I'm
untethered! Untied!
There's a whole
house to
roam!

Toothpaste Art

I'm magnificent stripes
of aqua and pink.
I make a masterpiece
in the sink.

Not Just Dental Floss

A bracelet.
A dog leash.
A jump rope!

The truth is
        I have
more fun
        without
a tooth.

Toilet Gets Bummed Out

Your fart jokes and sound effects stink!
You're just so funny—you *think*.

I flush and pretend I don't mind,
'cause I'm cold when you leave me, behind.

Pencil Plunge

We line up in sharp-pointed pairs.
We race from the top of the stairs.
We
       bump
           and
                we
                    jump.
We THUMP-ety THUMP!
Then we take a short break for repairs.

Mixed-Up Mixing Bowl

I tilt and twirl
a blurry swirl
I spin into
a tizzy

I wobble, sway
a bowl ballet—

oopsy!

Now I'm
dizzy

Revenge of the Lunchbox

I shuffle softly.
Sneak up.
Pause.

There's that monster
ball of claws.

I unzip teeth
and open wide

and catch that scratchy
cat inside!

21

Oh, My Aching Basketball!

You
    dribbled
        lots

Made
    awesome **s h o t S**

I
  pounded
      floor
My
  head
    is
      sore

I sleep in ice

  Ahhhhh

This . . . feels . . . nice . . .

Spaghetti Tries to Fit In

You left me there
       inside the bowl.
           Rejected!
For a garlic roll!

I long to be
      a thing you use!
         I lace myself
into your shoes.

23

Fruit Un-Rollup

I unroll
        (Stretchy. Sticky.)
to make a racetrack
        (Berry tricky.)

Vroom-Zoom-Stuck!

My wheels attack
the berry track.
The tricky snack
is long and steep.

Oh, no!
I'm stuck in berry muck.
I'm out of luck—
BEEP! BEEEEEEEEEEEP!

Shoes for All Seasons: *A Poem for Two Voices*

Flip Flops

I'm hidden away
all winter long.

To walk in wet snows . . .

Why is

winter

out of reach?

What's it like
to slide across ice?

I'd love the thrill of
cold, deep chill.

**I'm stuck in one season,
and that's no fair!
I want to feel**

winter

weather!

Let's try to escape

Let's run away

together!

Winter Boots

I've never seen
the beach.

To cuddle bare toes!

summer

Does hot sand
warm your sole?

I long for a
sunny stroll.

summer

and sample the seasons

Ready to Rock? No

End of day = time to play
But I admit: I like to sit

I'd Rather Stick With You

I'm lonely without my girl . . .

I'm a magic wand without a magician,
electric guitar without a musician.

I'm lonely without my girl . . .

I'm a bronco without a cowhand to ride me,
a sidekick without my hero beside me.

I'm lonely without my girl . . .

I want some adventure—to play and to laugh,
but nighttime's no fun when I'm only a half.

I'm lonely without my girl!

A Hose Unwinds After a Long Day

I lurk in a circle out on the lawn.
I'm a puddle of darkness—a great round yawn.

I'm a hoop. I'm a loop. I unwind and flow.
I'm a serpent skulking in shadowy glow.

I roll like a marble through thick green grass.
I'm the color of turtles and smooth sea glass.

My show is pure magic, here and then gone.
I curl in a circle just before dawn.

Good (?) Morning! *A Poem for Two Voices*

It's dawn!

          The sun shines fiery bright.

Our fun is done.

          Farewell, dark night!

We're worn out. *Whew.*

          We need a break.

But there's work to do.

          You're wide . . .

AWAKE!

For Maddie and Annabelle, my two favorite insomniacs
–LPS

For all the night owls creating by the light of the moon,
and much love to my supportive family and friends
–AM

WordSong
An Imprint of Highlights
815 Church Street
Honesdale, Pennsylvania 18431
wordsongpoetry.com
Printed in China

ISBN: 978-1-62091-630-8
Library of Congress Control Number: 2018943015

First edition
10 9 8 7 6 5 4 3 2 1

Design by Anahid Hamparian
The text and titles are set in Cabin and Mountains of Christmas.
The illustrations were painted mostly in the hours after dark, with acrylics, gouache,
and a touch of colored pencil on wood board.